Layla the Last Black Unicorn

Written by Tiffany Haddish & Jerdine Nolen

Illustrated by Jessica Gibson

HARPER

An Imprint of HarperCollinsPublishers

ISBN 978-0-06-311387-9

The artist used Photoshop and Procreate
to create the digital illustrations for this book.
Typography by Rachel Zegar
22 23 24 25 26 PC 10 9 8 7 6 5 4 3 2 1
❖
First Edition

For all of us finding our place to fit in
—J. N.

To my awesome supporting family
—J. G.

Layla loved summertime in the Overlook Woods. She loved having nothing to do but explore every nook and cranny of the forest.

Along with her friends
Gwendolyn Goblin, Olivia Fairy,
and Celia Cat, Layla would spend
her days searching the highest
branches of the mumsin trees
for the sweetest hanging fruit,

chasing sprites until she was
too tired to move,

and exploring every twist and turn in Melvin Minotaur's Maze.

But at this summer's end, things were different. As soon as the first leaf fell, Layla knew it was time to start going to school.

Layla lived in the heart of the forest with Trevin Troll. Trevin had watched over her and cared for her since Layla was barely old enough to trot on her own. He was kind and silly and had a laugh that could shake the clouds.

"Do I really have to go to school tomorrow?" Layla asked Trevin as he tucked her in for the night.

"Everybody has to go to school, Layla. It's nothing to be scared of. It's where you start to show the world how truly special you are."

"But . . . I'm not ready," Layla argued.

"Yes, you are," Trevin said, smiling as he tickled her behind her ear. "Trust me, she ready."

The next morning, Layla put on a brave smile as she first stepped through the grand gates of Unicornia. As she peered into the main courtyard, she thought she was in a dream. There were unicorns everywhere.

On the blacktop, a group of unicorns was playing Horn Ball while they waited for the first bell to ring.

"That's a two-fer, Peachy Pink," a blue unicorn said.

"No way, Babsy!" a rose-colored unicorn shot back. "It totally missed, so it's a dunkster. You lose a turn." Babsy seemed to know her friend was right, so she lowered her horn and stepped out of the circle.

The ball started to whiz around again as one unicorn after another slapped, whapped, and kicked it.

Layla tried to keep up with the action, but it was all moving too fast. That said, the game did look like a lot of fun, so when the ball skipped out and rolled over to her, Layla tried to throw it back, but . . .

POP!

"Hey, newbie—you just wrecked the game,"
Babsy said.

"It was an accident," Layla tried to explain.
"I didn't know the rules. We don't play Horn
Ball in Overlook Woods."

"Oh," Peachy said, shaking her head.
"Newbie's just . . . woodsy."

All the other unicorns laughed as the
last bell rang to start the day.

Unfortunately for Layla, things did not get much better from there:

she got lost on the way to her homeroom,

had no one to eat with at lunch,

and sat in someone's chewed gum during recess.

If this was her showing off how special she was, Layla would just as soon have hidden behind a mumsin tree for the rest of eternity.

But she knew she had to go back again the next day, and she was determined to find a way to fit in. Layla asked her friend Olivia Fairy to do her mane so it was awesome all over. Gwendolyn Goblin showered glitter around her legs and hooves. And Celia Cat made bows out of leaves and beads out of beetles.

"Now, she ready!" Layla sang as she danced a little dance.

But when Layla stepped off the bus the next morning, Babsy Baby Blue took one look at her and said, "Oh my . . . bows and beads and bangles and glitter. This girl is so very woodsy."

By the third day, Layla didn't want to go back to school at all. Finally, Trevin knocked on her bedroom door. "You're going to be late, Layla."

"I'm not going," Layla shot back. "I hate Unicornia. Everyone there calls me woodsy."

"Woodsy?" Trevin laughed that wonderful honking laugh of his. "If I had an ingot for every time someone called me 'woodsy,' I'd be one rich troll." Layla buried her head farther under her pillow. "They just don't know how special you are yet, Layla. Just be ready, and I promise, your time to shine will come."

Later, at the bus stop, Layla imagined having Trevin on one shoulder, Gwendolyn on the other, and placed Olivia and Celia in her heart. No matter how mean the other unicorns were, no one could take away what she had inside.

That day, Mrs. Carasom arranged a walking field trip into the Fiddle Dee Deep Forest.

Mrs. Carasom partnered up with Layla as they wandered into the woods. But she was so busy looking at her compass, cantering along, talking about the beauties of the world around them, that...

. . . she didn't notice there was a large patch of Devil's Shoestring and Ouchie Wowchie Shrubs right in front of her.

"Oh my, dearie me!" Mrs. Carasom cried.

"Bumbledy-shocks and fiddly-hocks. My foot . . . It's trapped."

"It's the shrub, Mrs. Carasom," Layla said, running over to the whispering willow tree. "I know how to get it to let go."

Layla gave a branch to each unicorn.

"Now do what I do!" she told the class. "Tickle the Ouchie Wowchie shrub."

"Tickle the plant?!" Babsy exclaimed. "Seriously?"

"It's the only way. Nothing can hurt you while it's laughing."

And much to the whole class's amazement, it worked!

Mrs. Carasom got up and dusted herself off, but when she bent down to get the things she'd dropped, she cried out, "Oh dear, no, my compass is broken."

"Don't worry, Mrs. Carasom. I grew up in these woods. We don't need a compass to find our way."

But then suddenly a huge thud shook the ground, and the woods around them grew dark.

"I'm scared." Babsy Baby Blue shuddered as the unicorns all clustered together. "I don't like the dark."

"Oh, you guys . . . there's nothing to fear," Layla told them as she turned around. "That's just Melvin Minotaur. We must have accidentally wandered near the entrance to his maze."

"Hey, Layla."

"Hey, Melvin." Layla smiled. "We're a little lost. Can you help us find our way back to school?"

"It'd be my pleasure," Melvin told her, before turning to the rest of the unicorns. "And you know, I used to be scared of the dark, too—before I met Layla, that is. Then I learned when something's black, it's really just where all the colors meet."

When they got back to school, Ms. Tulip, the principal, was waiting for them.

"Layla, you're a hero!" she exclaimed.

"Nah," Layla explained and smiled. "It's just how I am. She ready," she told her teacher as she did her little dance.

"She ready. She ready!"